JUSTINE McKEEN
QUEEN of GREEN

Sigmund Brouwer
illustrated by **Dave Whamond**

ORCA BOOK PUBLISHERS

To Barbara Kidd,
the Green Queen at Arthur Public School.
And a big thank you to two of the greenest families I know:
Ivan, Selena, Sydney and Adam Hucal;
and Morris, Lesia, Myra, Adrian and Kalynna Hucal

Text copyright © 2011 Sigmund Brouwer
Illustrations copyright © 2011 Dave Whamond

Library and Archives Canada Cataloguing in Publication

Brouwer, Sigmund, 1959-
Justine McKeen, queen of green / Sigmund Brouwer ;
illustrated by Dave Whamond.
(Orca echoes)

Issued also in electronic format.
ISBN 978-1-55469-927-8

I. Whamond, Dave II. Title. III. Series: Orca echoes
PS8553.R68467J88 2011   JC813'.54   C2011-903476-X

First published in the United States, 2011
Library of Congress Control Number: 2011929400

Summary: Justine and her friends are all about being green and helping the planet,
one environmental project at time.

Orca Book Publishers gratefully acknowledges the support for its publishing programs
provided by the following agencies: the Government of Canada through the Canada Book
Fund and the Canada Council for the Arts, and the Province of British Columbia
through the BC Arts Council and the Book Publishing Tax Credit.

MIX
Paper from
responsible sources
FSC® C016245

*Orca Book Publishers is dedicated to preserving the environment and has printed this book
on paper certified by the Forest Stewardship Council®.*

Cover artwork and interior illustrations by Dave Whamond
Author photo by Reba Baskett

ORCA BOOK PUBLISHERS   ORCA BOOK PUBLISHERS
PO Box 5626, Stn. B   PO Box 468
Victoria, BC Canada   Custer, WA USA
V8R 6S4   98240-0468

www.orcabook.com
Printed and bound in Canada.

14 13 12 11 • 4 3 2 1

Chapter One

Justine McKeen sat at a table in the school lunchroom with her two new friends, Safdar and Michael. It was noisy and busy, as usual. The older kids were leaving to make room for the kids in Justine's class.

"Did you see that?" Justine said. "The guy in the blue hoodie just threw an empty can in the garbage."

"The guy in the blue hoodie is the meanest guy in the school," Safdar said. "He is older and bigger than us too. He can do whatever he wants."

"Yeah," Michael said. "His name is Jimmy Blatzo. Never, ever call him Fatso Blatzo."

"That empty can should have gone in the recycling," Justine said.

She set her backpack on the table. She ran toward two older students who were clearing their lunch trays off into the garbage. They stared at Justine as she reached into the garbage can.

Safdar looked at Michael. "If she's that hungry, maybe we should give her some of our lunch."

Michael poked the food on his tray with his fork. "She's a fast learner. Only a couple of days at this school, and already she knows garbage tastes better than cafeteria food."

"Ha, ha," said Safdar.

"Who was joking?" Michael said.

Justine was holding a juice can and some papers. She stepped toward the recycling bins. She threw the juice in one and the papers in another.

She joined Safdar and Michael. "I'll be right back. I need to wash my hands. You know, there was a lot of stuff in the garbage that would be great for a compost. What do you think, guys?"

"That we're in trouble," Michael said.

"For wanting to recycle?" she asked.

"No," Michael said, "because here comes the guy in the blue hoodie. Jimmy Blatzo. Please, please don't call him Fatso Blatzo."

Chapter Two

"What's your name?" Jimmy Blatzo asked Justine. He towered over her and looked angry.

"Justine McKeen," she said. She stuck out a hand and waited for him to shake it. Her hand had mustard on it. "Nice to meet you, Jimmy Blatzo."

He pushed her hand away. "I heard you dug in the garbage for my empty juice can. You made me look bad. Is that what you wanted? Because I don't like being made to look bad."

"You look like my cousin Joe," Justine said. "He lives in Detroit. Detroit is an amazing city. Cars. Lots of cars. Now they are building electric cars there. Isn't that great? It will really help the environment.

I would like a blue one someday. Like the color of your hoodie. That's a nice hoodie. What's the picture on the front of your hoodie? Is it—?"

"Are you listening to me?" Jimmy Blatzo said. He crossed his arms and took a step forward. "You made me look bad."

"The picture on your hoodie looks like the wings of a bird," she said. "If you moved your arms, I could see it better. And maybe stand back a little. I hope it's a bird. Birds are cool. We have birds in our backyard. Cardinals. Blue jays. Even—"

Jimmy Blatzo's face turned very red. "Enough!" His head looked like a tomato that was about to burst.

"Maybe we should go," Safdar said. He stood and handed Justine her backpack. Michael stood too. Safdar and Michael took a couple of steps back.

"Maybe you shouldn't!" Jimmy Blatzo said. He grabbed Justine's backpack and dumped the contents out on the table. He grabbed her lunch bag

and dumped it out on the table too. He grabbed her juice box, drank it and set it down. "Recycle this!"

"Always," Justine said. "Reduce. Reuse. Recycle. That's me. Did you know a faucet that leaks a drop of water every ten seconds loses nearly forty gallons of water a month? If it's a hot-water faucet, it's even worse because of the energy it takes to heat the water. And lights. Don't get me started on turning lights off. Everywhere. All the time. And—"

"Who are you?" Blatzo said. He squashed her sandwich with his fist. "The Queen of Green?"

"I like that," she said. "Justine McKeen, Queen of Green. Wow. Thank you. And I also like what you did with my sandwich. You turned it into pita bread. Thanks." She stuck out her hand again to say goodbye. "It was nice to meet you, Blatzo. I hope you're not late for class."

"You don't understand," he said. "You made me look bad. I'm not letting you get away with this. And don't call me by my last name!"

Jimmy Blatzo saw Justine's brownies in a ziplock bag on the table. He grabbed the squares. "This is your punishment."

He pulled out a brownie and crammed it into his mouth.

"May I have the bag back?" Justine asked. "Reduce. Reuse. Recycle."

"Not a chance," he said, chewing. He marched out of the cafeteria.

"That's too bad," Justine told Michael and Safdar.

"What?" Safdar asked. "That you made enemies with the biggest bully in the school?"

"Or that he drank your juice, smashed your sandwiches and took your dessert?" said Michael.

"No," said Justine, "he took the ziplock bag. I was hoping to use it for the whole school year. Plus, those brownies were part of my science project."

Chapter Three

After lunch, Mrs. Howie waited for her students to be seated.

"It's time for a science presentation," Mrs. Howie said. She ran her finger down the list of names on her desk. "Justine, today is your turn. Do you have something to present to the class?"

"Yes!" Justine said.

"Good," Mrs. Howie said. "Come up to the front, and remember, introducing yourself is part of a good presentation."

Justine walked to the back of the classroom and grabbed the posters she had made. She marched to the front and turned to face everyone.

"Hello," she said. "My name is Justine McKeen. But I won't mind if you call me Justine McKeen, Queen of Green. Somebody gave me that name in the cafeteria today, and I like it. It is very important to be green, and my science project today is about how we can help the environment. I want to start by showing you a poster of a cow from Argentina."

Justine held up her first poster. It was of a black and white cow with a huge pink tank strapped to its back. The tank was tube-shaped. It stretched from the cow's head to its tail.

"This tank is made from the same kind of plastic as a beach ball," Justine said. "And the tank is filled with something lighter than air. It is filled with a gas called methane. The tank collects methane from the cow's body."

Safdar put up his hand. "Yes, Safdar," Mrs. Howie said.

"Miss Queen of Green," Safdar said. "I thought cows made milk. Not methane."

"I don't want to be rude," Justine said, "but I will explain a different way. The tank collects the gas from the cow's F-A-R-Ts."

"Cow F-A-R-Ts!" Safdar said. "Cool! I vote that this is the best science project ever!"

Michael put up his hand.

Mrs. Howie had a tired look on her face. She sounded tired when she spoke too. "Yes, Michael."

Michael stood. "Miss Queen of Green, how does the tank collect the cow F-A-R-Ts?"

"Please call it methane," Justine said. "We should use the scientific word."

"Cool!" Michael said. "Cow F-A-R-Ts. Do you have a photo of the cow's hind end? Is there a tube in the cow's butt to collect the F-A-R-Ts?"

Everyone laughed.

Mrs. Howie stepped forward. "Class!"

Nobody was listening. They were laughing too hard.

"Class!" Mrs. Howie shouted. "Please, let Justine continue!"

"Thank you," Justine said. "It is important for scientists to know how much methane a cow produces. Methane contributes to global warming. Argentina has fifty-five million cows. One cow produces one thousand quarts of methane a day. That is a lot of methane. Since farmers care about the environment, they want to know if there is a way to feed cows so the cows produce less gas."

Michael put up his hand again.

"No," Mrs. Howie said, "we don't have time for another question about cow gas."

"Rats," Michael said.

Justine held up a poster of a hamburger. "I'm glad farmers raise cows, because I love to eat these." She pointed at the poster. "But it would be cool if farmers raised crickets too. Insects are good protein. Farmers could have cow ranches

15

and cricket ranches. Fewer cow ranches means less methane in the air."

"I LOVE this project!" Michael said. "Cow F-A-R-Ts and bug eating!"

Mrs. Howie coughed. "No more interruptions, please, class."

Justine held up a poster of a cricket. "In Japan, many people eat this insect. I added crickets into melted chocolate to make brownies. I was going to share them with the class. The bad news is someone ate that part of my project in the cafeteria today. The good news is he seemed to like it."

Chapter Four

"Hey, Justine, Queen of Green," Safdar said as he and Michael sat down for lunch the next day. "There's something you should know about Ice-Cream Heaven."

"Yum," Michael said. "Any ice cream is heaven to me."

"Seriously," Safdar said. "Yesterday, I saw the owner throwing all his recyclables into a Dumpster."

"What!" Justine stood. "I've been to Ice-Cream Heaven with my grammy. There are different recycle bins out front. If he didn't recycle, Grammy and I wouldn't go there."

"I know," Safdar said. "But I saw him emptying the bins in the regular garbage out back. I asked him why, and he said it was too much work to recycle. He said he only has recycle bins in front of his shop to make him look good."

"*Arrgg,*" Justine said.

"Is *arrgg* a word?" Michael asked. He poked at the food on his cafeteria tray. "If so, I think that's what we were served today."

"I told the owner that what he was doing was wrong," Safdar said. "You know what he said?"

"What?" Justine asked.

"Next time he'll make sure to do his garbage dumping at night, when smarty pants like me can't see him. Maybe we should start a petition for all the kids in school to sign against Ice-Cream Heaven. Then make signs and march back and forth in his parking lot. That would serve him right for not being green."

"*Arrgg*," Justine said again. She looked at Michael. "If I want *arrgg* to be a word, it's a word. After all, I am the queen."

"You just got the name yesterday," Michael said. "And you are only the Queen of Green. Not the whole Earth."

"If you care about the Earth, then you care about green," she said. "And if you care about green, then you care about the Earth. So if I'm the Queen of Green, then maybe I am the Queen of—"

"Oh no," Safdar said. "Watch out. Here's comes Jimmy Blatzo."

"Remember," Michael said to Justine, "don't call him Fatso Blatzo."

Jimmy Blatzo walked up and stood in front of them.

"Hey, Queen of Green," he said. "I want to talk to you about those brownies I ate yesterday. They were really good but different."

"It was probably the crickets I mixed in with the chocolate," Justine said.

"Crickets?" Blatzo said. His eyebrows furrowed. He was angry again.

"Yes, crickets. I believe we should all eat insects. It will help the environment. My grammy and I made more cricket brownies last night. After you ate my first batch, I didn't have any to share with my class."

"*Arrgg*," Michael said.

"Nice try," Blatzo told Justine.

"I'm glad you appreciate my brownies," she said. "Lots of people think I'm weird for making cricket brownies."

"*Arrgg*," Michael said again.

"I mean nice try to stop me from taking more of them," Blatzo said. "Crickets. Right! As if I would believe that. You can't fool me."

He grabbed her backpack and opened it. When he found the ziplock bag of brownies, he yanked it out and opened it. He stuffed a brownie in his mouth.

"Make sure you bring me more brownies tomorrow," he said as he chewed. "Or else."

"Sure," Justine said. "But can you give me back the bag so I can use it again?"

Chapter Five

"Hello, Mr. Tait," Justine said. She was at the front of the line at Ice-Cream Heaven. "My name is Justine McKeen. Some people call me the Queen of Green."

"That's nice," Mr. Tait said in the way adults sometimes speak so kids will stop pestering them. He was a short man with a round head. He wore an apron with a name tag. "What would you like to order?"

"A small corner of your parking lot," Justine said.

"What?" he said. "Are you the Queen of Green or the Queen of Crazy? I can't give you a piece of my parking lot."

"It's for a school fundraiser," Justine said. "On a Saturday. Three weeks from now."

"What kind of fundraiser?" he asked. "Not a car wash. The kids from the high school had a car wash in my parking lot once, and it was too noisy."

"It's a vegetable-selling fundraiser," she said. "Fresh vegetables. Made the green way."

"Only one way to make vegetables," he said. "Put seeds in dirt."

"That's only part of it," she said. "You also shouldn't use pesticides or chemicals. You see, there are natural ways to keep bugs off vegetables. All you do is—"

"What's your name?" Mr. Tait said.

"Justine McKeen, Queen of Green."

"Look, Miss Queen of Green," Mr. Tait said. "I'm not interested in all this talk about green or in letting you use my parking lot."

"What if we give you half of the money we raise as rent?"

"Well, that changes things," he said. "Okay, you can rent a corner of my parking lot to sell your green vegetables. Just don't waste my time with all this talk about green. People talk about green this and green that because it makes them feel good. The rest of us have jobs to do."

"Thank you, Mr. Tait," Justine said. "By the way, if you are ever interested in putting cricket brownies on your menu, they make a good dessert. Just ask Jimmy Blatzo."

"*Arrgg*," Mr. Tait said.

"I knew *arrgg* was a word," Justine said to herself as she walked out of Ice-Cream Heaven.

Chapter Six

Outside Ice-Cream Heaven, Michael and Safdar were waiting for Justine beside their bicycles.

"Mr. Tait told you he wouldn't do it," Michael said. "Right? I mean, it is a crazy idea."

"Actually," Justine said, "Mr. Tait said it would be okay."

"Huh?" Michael said.

Safdar put up his hand, as if he was sitting in class.

"Yes, Safdar," Justine said, as if she were his teacher.

"Did you tell Mr. Tait exactly what your idea was?" Safdar asked. "Because I think if he knew

exactly what you wanted to do, there's no way he would have agreed."

"I told him most of what we were going to do," Justine said.

"Most?" Michael asked.

"Most," she said. "Some things you can't spring on people all at once. That's what my grammy says. This was partly her idea, you know."

"To build a—," said Michael.

"No," Justine said, "not to build our project. But to find a way to get Mr. Tait to be more green. My grammy said when you criticize people, it only makes them defend what they are doing, so it's harder to change their habits. She said it's much easier to get people on your side by asking them for help. So instead of a petition and marching back and forth with signs in protest, I thought we should let Mr. Tait help us build a wonderful green project in his parking lot."

"Great," Michael said. "And in case you are wondering, by great, I mean not so great."

"It will be fine," Justine said. "There's only one thing we need to do. Over the next three weeks, we need our class to help us collect fifteen hundred empty plastic soda bottles."

"Fifteen hundred?" Safdar said. "Like one thousand five hundred?"

"Sure," Justine said. "Great ideas take work, you know."

"I have only one word for this," Michael said.

Safdar and Justine looked at him.

"*Arrgg*," he said.

Chapter Seven

Two weeks later, Michael and Safdar followed Justine home after school. She lived with her grandmother.

"Hi, Grammy," Justine said. "These are my friends, Michael and Safdar. They are going to help me make posters."

Grammy smiled. Judging from the wrinkles on her face, the boys could tell she smiled a lot.

"Hello, boys," she said. "I'm glad you are helping Justine with her green project. I hear your class has collected almost fifteen hundred plastic bottles."

"Yes, we have," Michael said. "Helping to make posters didn't sound all that fun, but Justine promised we could use power tools."

"Yeah," Safdar said, "power tools. Boys LIKE power tools."

"What I said about the power tools is mostly true," said Justine.

"Mostly?" Safdar said.

"Yes," Justine said. "Remember what I told you before. Some things you can't spring on people all at once. You are here now, so even if we don't need to use power tools, there's no point going home. Right?"

"*Arrgg*," Michael said. He was beginning to think *arrgg* was a good word.

"Don't worry," Justine said. "When I said power tools, I was talking about a paper shredder, a blender and a hair dryer."

"Cool," Safdar said. "I LIKE power tools. Any kind of power tools."

"But first," Grammy said, "Justine needs to do something about our maggots."

"Maggots?" Michael said.

"Little white worms that turn into flies," Justine said. "They are really good for wounds that are infected. You put maggots on a wound and they eat all the decaying flesh."

"Nice," Michael said. "And by nice, I mean not so nice."

"Follow me," Justine said.

She took Michael and Safdar into the garage. There was a big plastic bucket on the floor. It had lots of holes drilled into it. It was filled with brown stuff. It wasn't smelly. But it had lots of little white things crawling around the top.

"This is our compost bin," Justine said. "Grammy and I throw our soft garbage into it. Things like vegetable peels and eggshells, coffee grounds and tea bags, scrapings from our plates and—"

"Getting the picture," Michael said.

"Later," she said, "we can use the compost as fertilizer. For the project at Ice-Cream Heaven."

Safdar leaned over and watched all the maggots squirming on top. "Cool! When do they turn into flies and fly away?"

"Oh, they will fly away." Justine laughed. "But they will have help."

She dragged the compost bin out of the garage and away from the house. She led Michael and Safdar back into the house where they could watch the bin from the front window.

"It should only take a minute," she said.

She was right. About a minute later, several birds swooped down and began pecking at the compost.

"See," she said. "The maggots *are* flying away. It's the natural way to get rid of pests."

Chapter Eight

"Are you ready to use the power tools now?" Justine asked. Safdar and Michael nodded. They were gathered around Justine's kitchen table.

"Exactly how does a blender and a hair dryer help us make a poster?" Safdar asked.

"Don't forget the paper shredder," Michael said.

"Easy," Justine said. "Maybe I should have mentioned all the shredding has been done."

"Let me guess," Michael said. "Some things you can't spring on people all at once."

"Wow," Justine said. "You ARE smart."

"*Arrgg,*" Michael said.

Justine smiled. She opened the closet and pulled out a bag of shredded paper. "First," she said, "we scoop shredded paper into a blender. Then we add warm water and put the lid on."

"Let's call it a POWER blender," Safdar said. "That will make me feel more grown-up."

Justine smiled again. "Safdar, can you hit the button on the POWER blender?"

When he did, the blender made a lot of loud, satisfying noises.

The three of them filled the blender ten times with shredded paper and water. They poured the mixture into a large plastic tub.

"Now what?" Michael asked.

"We pour it into a mold and deckle," Justine said. She pointed at something that looked like an old window frame with a metal screen. "Then we drain the water off into the tub."

When she had finished, she lifted the mold off and flipped the deckle over onto the old sheet that covered the kitchen table. Then she lifted the deckle off.

"Now we sponge off any extra water," she said. There was a large square piece of mushy paper on the table. "Finally, we use the hair dryer."

"That would be the POWER hair dryer," Safdar said.

"Of course," she said.

Safdar dried the paper with the hair dryer. Altogether, they made eight sheets of recycled paper.

"Excellent," she said. "Now we have paper for our posters and compost to fertilize the soil for the Ice-Cream Heaven project. This way we can tell the woman from the newspaper the entire project is green."

"Newspaper?" Michael said. "I don't remember hearing anything about a newspaper reporter."

"I thought you had learned," Justine said. "Some things you can't spring on people all at once."

Chapter Nine

The Saturday morning they had been waiting for finally arrived. It was sunny and warm. Most of their class had showed up at the Ice-Cream Heaven parking lot to help.

Several parents had delivered the materials. They brought lumber, thin wooden poles and bags and bags of empty plastic bottles. They also had buckets with warm water and wheelbarrows of dirt.

"Where is Mr. Tait, the owner?" Mrs. Howie asked.

"He usually gets here in the afternoon," Justine said. "It would be great to have our project set up before he arrives. It will be a big surprise!"

Safdar whispered to Michael, "Yes, some things you can't spring on people all at once."

"That's not our biggest problem," Michael said. "Look who is watching us."

Jimmy Blatzo stood at the corner of the parking lot.

"Let me guess," Safdar said. "Better not call him Fatso Blazto."

"Exactly," Michael said.

Justine saw Jimmy Blatzo too. "Remember, when you criticize people they get defensive, it's better to ask them for their help."

She waved at Jimmy Blatzo. "Hey, Blatzo," she shouted, "get your butt over here."

Jimmy Blatzo stomped toward Justine.

"Don't just stand there looking angry," she said. "You are strong and smart. We need you to help Michael and Safdar nail the frame together."

"Why should I help you, Miss Queen of Green?"

"Because we can't do it without you. We need your strength."

Jimmy Blatzo was so surprised, he picked up a hammer and started nailing lumber planks together with Safdar.

"This would be much easier," Jimmy Blatzo said, "if we had power tools."

"Ooooh," Safdar said, "power tools." He gave Jimmy a high five. They laughed and started back to work.

At school the day before, Justine had explained to her classmates what everyone's jobs were.

Some students nailed boards together in the shape of a giant sandbox.

Some soaked bottles in water to remove the labels.

Some filled the giant sandbox with dirt and mixed in the compost for fertilizer.

Some planted vegetable seeds.

Some cut the bottoms off the plastic bottles.

Some slid the bottles onto thin wooden poles.

A few hours later, the project was almost finished, except for one thing. They needed someone big to put the roof on.

"Hey, Blatzo," Justine said. "Get your butt over here."

"What is it now?" he asked.

"You are strong and smart," she said. "We need to put you in charge of the roof."

Jimmy Blatzo did all the heavy lifting. A couple of minutes later, the roof was finished.

"Ta-da!" Justine said. "A greenhouse!"

Mr. Tait pulled into Ice-Cream Heaven's parking lot. He parked his car and stomped toward Justine. "What is this?" he said. "You told me you were having a vegetable sale."

"We are," she said. "It just might take awhile for the vegetables to grow. They are inside the greenhouse right now. As seeds."

"A plastic-bottle greenhouse?" he said.

"Reduce. Reuse. Recycle," she said. "That's only one of the reasons they call me the Queen of Green."

"That's where you are wrong," he said. "Your name has been changed to the Queen of Take It Down Right Now."

Chapter Ten

A woman rushed up to Justine and Mr. Tait. She had a small tape recorder in one hand and a camera in her other hand.

"Hello, Mr. Tait," the woman said. "My name is Lily Kempler. I'm from the newspaper. I'm glad you are here. I wanted to talk to you about all this."

"This? This?" Mr. Tait said. "Did someone complain about it already?" Mr. Tait leaned over and whispered in Justine's ear so only she could hear. "You will pull it down immediately!"

"This is an amazing project. Who would complain?" Lily Kempler said. "It's wonderful that you would encourage kids to make a greenhouse out of empty soda bottles. And it's great advertising, don't you think?"

"Well…," Mr. Tait said.

"Yes, it's great advertising," Justine said. "And it's important to be green. I'm glad Mr. Tait is green, aren't you Mr. Tait?"

"Well…" Mr. Tait rubbed his forehead.

"I want to take a photo of you with the kids," Lily Kempler said. "For the newspaper. I think this should be on the front page. Would that be okay with you, Mr. Tait?"

Mr. Tait sighed. "Well…"

"Maybe we could stand over there beside one of the posters about the project," Justine said. "The posters are made from recycled paper. The fertilizer for the greenhouse is made from a home composter. No chemicals. This is as green as green can be. And when we sell the vegetables, we can use the money toward another green project. Right, Mr. Tait?"

"Well…," Mr. Tait said.

Justine took his hand and dragged him toward the greenhouse. She pulled so hard that he leaned forward. "Mr. Tait," Justine whispered in his ear. "If we stand over there, the Ice-Cream Heaven sign will be in the photo. Free advertising. On the front page."

Mr. Tait looked at the sign. "Well…"

"Safdar!" Justine called. "Michael! Over here."

She looked at Lily Kempler. "It's only fair if my friends are in the photo too. They did a lot of work." Justine stood on one side of Mr. Tait. Michael and Safdar stood on the other side.

"Ready?" Lily Kempler asked. She pointed her camera at them.

"Almost," Justine said. She shouted again. "Hey, Blatzo, get your butt over here."

Jimmy Blatzo lumbered over. "What?"

"Come stand beside me," she said.

"Are you always going to order me around?" he said.

"I *am* the Queen of Green," she said. "Besides, I'll bring more cricket brownies to school on Monday for you."

"Say cheese!" Lily Kempler said.

"No," Mr. Tait said. "Say ice cream!"

Everyone grinned. There was a flash as Lily Kempler snapped the photo.

"So, Mr. Tait," she said and held out her tape recorder. "How long will the greenhouse be here? I'm sure folks are going to be talking about it. They will be very proud of your community spirit."

"I don't know how long it will be up," Mr. Tait said. "Why don't we let this girl tell you? In fact, she can answer all your questions about the project, right?"

"Right," Justine said to Mr. Tait. She pulled the tape recorder close to her mouth and spoke into it. "First, my name is spelled J-U-S-T-I-N-E M-C-K-E-E-N. Justine McKeen."

"Yes," Mr. Tait said to Lily Kempler. "Justine McKeen. But you should call her the Queen of Green."

Chapter Eleven

On Monday at lunch, Justine sat in the cafeteria with Michael and Safdar.

Safdar removed his science project from his backpack. His project used two big soda bottles. He was about to explain what it was when Justine saw Jimmy Blatzo leaving the cafeteria with the older kids.

"Hey, Blatzo," she yelled. She stood and waved at him. "How are you doing?"

He frowned and shook his head at her. He raised a finger in front of his mouth and made a shushing sound.

"Hey, Blatzo, you looked good in the newspaper!" she shouted.

Jimmy Blazto marched up to her table. "Come on," he said. "You can't yell at me like we're friends or something. And don't call me by my last name. If I let you get away with doing it, people will stop being scared of me."

"*I'm* scared of you," Michael said.

"Me too," Safdar said. "Really scared." Safdar clutched his science project bottles close.

"Blatzo," Justine said. "That's stupid. Why do you need people to be scared of you?"

He shrugged.

"Exactly, there's no good reason at all," Justine said. "Besides, I bet it felt great to help us on Saturday. We needed someone strong and smart." Justine opened her backpack and handed him a ziplock bag. "I brought you the cricket brownies as promised. It took me awhile to catch more crickets."

"Ha, ha. Yeah, sure it did," Jimmy Blatzo said. He took out the brownies. He chewed on one and handed back the empty bag. "Reduce. Reuse. Recycle. Right?"

"Right," Justine said.

Jimmy Blatzo swallowed a big bite of brownie. "Boy, these sure make me thirsty." He looked at Safdar. "Give me some of that soda."

Safdar pulled the bottles closer.

"I should have asked nicer," Jimmy Blatzo said. "Please could you give me some?"

"That's not a good idea," Safdar said.

"I thought you said you were scared of me." Blatzo grabbed one of the bottles. "Ginger ale?"

"No," Safdar said. "It's my science project. It's a fire extinguisher. Instead of chemicals that are bad for the environment, the bottles have lemon juice mixed with baking soda."

"Ha, ha," Jimmy Blatzo said. "One of you tells me there are crickets in the brownies. The other one says his soda is a fire extinguisher. Remember, you can't fool someone like me."

"Please don't tip the bottle," Safdar said.

"Like this?" Jimmy Blatzo said. He lifted the bottle and tilted it toward himself.

Nothing happened.

"See?" Jimmy Blatzo said. "You can't fool me."

He started to take off the lid.

The lid popped off and hit him in the nose. Foam sprayed all over him.

"What's this?" he shouted.

"I told you," Safdar said. "A fire extinguisher."

"I'm going to give you to the count of three before I grab all of you!" Jimmy Blatzo shouted.

Michael and Safdar dropped their lunches and ran.

"Hey," Jimmy Blatzo said to Justine. His shirt and pants were soaked. "How come you're still here?"

"Sit your butt down, Blatzo," she said. "I'm here because we need to talk. You're going to help me with my next project. I'm thinking we need a garden on the roof of the school."

JUSTINE McKEEN
QUEEN of GREEN

Notes for Students and Teachers

Chapter Two

Green projects are a lot of fun, and I hope this book gives you some ideas for how you can pitch in. It's just as important, though, to do small things that no one would probably notice. The biggest difference kids can make is doing small acts every day, such as taking home the ziplock bag from your lunch to use the next day, or using cold water instead of hot, or checking the taps for drips. These small acts of conservation may seem boring, but if all of us do them, the impact is huge.

Chapter Three
Cow F-A-R-Ts

Farmers are among the most responsible people when it comes to the environment. Part of why they choose to farm is because they love the land.

They care about the environment because they depend on the environment every day. Justine didn't make up the story about scientists and cow F-A-R-Ts. More information and research on cow methane can be found on the Internet.

But watch out! If you google *cow farts*, you'll probably find a couple of links to cow farts in a can. Yes, people who move to the city and miss the smell of the country can buy cow farts in a can.

Chapter Four
Insects as human food!

Do you think *Insects as Food* would be a fun report to present to your class? As Justine points out, people in many different cultures eat insects. If you would like to learn more about it, or to write a report guaranteed to gross out your class (and your teacher!), there is lots of information on the Internet. To get started, enter *food + insects* into Google or any other search engine.

Chapter Five

My family loves local produce. It tastes fresher, and we know buying local reduces our carbon footprint because we are not buying produce that has been shipped from across the country or the other side of the world. A carbon footprint is the sum of all emissions of carbon dioxide (CO_2) a person's activities create in a given time frame.

Chapter Seven

Two words: Compost bin.

    Three words: Easy to do.

    Four words: Makes a big difference.

    More words: Jump on the Internet and learn how easy home compost bins are to set up. (By the way, I learned from friends about how to get rid of the maggots in my own compost bin.)

Chapter Eight

The Internet has lots of information on how to recycle paper and use it for cool art projects. And remember, paper shredders, blenders and hair dryers really are POWER TOOLS!!

Chapter Nine

There are a lot of links on the Internet to show you how to build a plastic-bottle greenhouse. I was particularly inspired by Rogart Primary School in Sutherland, Scotland, and their greenhouse project.

Chapter Eleven

Do you want to make an environmentally friendly fire extinguisher for a science project? (Just remember, it's not for grease or electrical fires.)

Here's what you need:

- a plastic bottle
- lemon juice or vinegar
- tissue
- rubber band
- baking soda

How do you put all of it together? Hint: enter *science project + fire extinguisher* into a search engine.

Sigmund Brouwer is the bestselling author of many books for children and young adults. Sigmund loves visiting schools and talking with youth of all ages about reading and writing. *Justine McKeen, Queen of Green* is the first book in his new series about Justine and her efforts to create a greener community. He also has a new book for teachers and parents called *Rock & Roll Literacy*. Sigmund lives in Red Deer, Alberta, and Nashville, Tennessee.